DE '98

Other books in the
Little Polar Bear series
by Hans de Beer

LITTLE POLAR BEAR

·

AHOY THERE, LITTLE POLAR BEAR

·

LITTLE POLAR BEAR FINDS A FRIEND

·

LITTLE POLAR BEAR, TAKE ME HOME!

Copyright © 1992, 1998 by Nord-Süd Verlag AG, Gossau Zürich, Switzerland.
First published in Switzerland under the title *Der kleine Eisbär und der Angsthase*.
English translation copyright © 1998 by North-South Books Inc.
Adapted from the easy-to-read edition of the same title.

First published in the United States, Great Britain, Canada,
Australia, and New Zealand in 1998 by North-South Books,
an imprint of Nord-Süd Verlag AG, Gossau Zürich, Switzerland.

Distributed in the United States by North-South Books Inc., New York.

Library of Congress Cataloging-in-Publication Data is available.
A CIP catalogue record for this book is available from The British Library.
ISBN 0-7358-1011-7 (TRADE BINDING)
1 3 5 7 9 TB 10 8 6 4 2
ISBN 0-7358-1012-5 (LIBRARY BINDING)
1 3 5 7 9 LB 10 8 6 4 2
Printed in Belgium

For more information about our books, and the authors and artists
who create them, visit our web site: http://www.northsouth.com

Little Polar Bear
and the Brave Little Hare

Written and Illustrated by
Hans de Beer

Translated by J. Alison James

North-South Books
New York / London

Lars, the little polar bear, lived at the North Pole. He liked to sit on a little hill and look out over the ice and snow to the sea.

Usually it was very quiet at the North Pole; the only sound was the wind. But one day Lars heard something else, a faint whimper. He turned his nose in the direction of the sound and sniffed. He smelled something unfamiliar. On silent paws, Lars followed the smell until he found a deep hole. The whimpering clearly came from down in the hole. What could it be?

Lars leaned nervously over the edge. Down at the bottom sat a small hare, shivering with fear.

"Don't be afraid," Lars said to him. "I will help you."

The little hare's eyes grew large as Lars pushed down a heap of snow, but then he understood, and with a hop-hop-hop he was free!

"I was so scared!" said the little hare.

"Everything is all right now," said Lars. "What's your name?"

"I'm Hugo," said the hare.

"My name's Lars. Come on, let's race!"

"Great!" cried Hugo, for he loved to race. And he certainly could run fast, so fast that he easily beat the little polar bear!

Soon it started to snow.

"When it snows, I have to go home," said Hugo. "My parents said so."

"That's too bad," said Lars. "But I'll walk you home."

It snowed harder and harder. The two struggled against the wind. The snow was so thick that they couldn't see a thing, so they snuggled up against each other and waited out the storm.

Finally it stopped snowing. The sky was bright and clear again. Lars and Hugo shook off all the snow. Everything looked different and strange.

"Where are we?" wailed Hugo. "We'll never find our way back home!"

"Don't worry, Hugo," said Lars. "I often get lost, but I always find my way home again."

"But I'm hungry," said Hugo.

Suddenly they heard a loud rattling noise. Something red was rumbling through the snow.

Hugo quickly burrowed into a pile of snow.

"You're such a scaredy-hare!" called Lars, laughing. "Come on out! That was only a car."

"A what?" asked Hugo from deep inside the snow.

"A car! It belongs to the polar station. My father takes me there all the time, and we find delicious things to eat! Come on! I know the way home from there."

Lars and Hugo followed the car's tracks. Soon they saw the polar station.

"Now that you know where we are," Hugo said. "Let's go straight home!" The polar station made him nervous.

"Don't be a scaredy-hare," said Lars. "Let's get something to eat first."

"I'm not so hungry now," said Hugo.

"I am," said Lars. "Wait until you see what good things they have to eat down there. Come on!"

When the car left again, Hugo gathered his courage and followed Lars down to the polar station. In the rubbish behind the station they found fish, bread, and two crunchy carrots — enough for a little picnic.

"I'm just going to take a look around," called Lars to the hare. "You can wait here if you want."

The little polar bear climbed up to the roof of the polar station. He noticed an opening that wasn't a door and wasn't a window. It had a funny smell. Lars heard an unusual noise. He wanted to get a closer look, so he pushed aside the grate and leaned into the opening. He still couldn't see, so he leaned in further and further . . . and then . . . oops!

Lars fell headfirst into the shaft, but luckily he landed—
PLOOF!—on a chair.

It was hot in the room. Everything bleeped and blinked in a
frightening way. Now Lars wanted to go home too! He looked
around and noticed a door. Quickly he slipped through and
looked for the way out. But all the doors to the outside were
locked. Lars was really scared now.

Lars paced through the rooms. Suddenly he had a shock—the car was returning. Any moment now the man would be here! Terrified, Lars searched for a hiding place.

Hugo also heard the car. He saw the man get out. I have to help Lars! thought Hugo. His heart pounded wildly. Fast as lightning, he hopped down to the polar station. But the man was already at the door. What now?

With springing leaps, Hugo jumped up to the roof. He heard noises through the shaft. The man is down there! thought Hugo. I have to save Lars. But how?

Then Hugo got an idea. He turned around and pushed with his hind feet. Snow plopped down the shaft. He kept pushing, as fast as he could.

The man looked up. "What is happening on the roof?" he said, and headed out to see what was going on. He didn't notice the little polar bear, but he *did* leave the door open.

Lars slipped out the door, and as soon as he saw that the coast was clear, he ran away as fast as he could.

"Come down, Hugo, quick!" he called from a safe distance. "I'm out. I'm over here!"

Hugo dashed between the man's legs, and took one great leap off the roof.

Lars and Hugo ran and ran, as fast as they could. It was just like a race. And Hugo was still faster.

"Wait for me!" cried Lars, out of breath. Hugo stopped. They were already quite far from the polar station.

"I was so scared!" said Lars. "But you were very brave. You saved me. Now you can call me a scaredy-bear."

"I wasn't brave," said Hugo. "I just did what I had to do. And everything is all right now."

Together they found their way home.